W9-AAT-286
Books
Give Us
Wings
99-00
SCPL
St. Charles Public Library
Family Read-Aloud Book Club
Presented in honor of:
The Wixted Family

The Crooked Apple Tree

written by Eric Houghton
illustrated by Caroline Gold

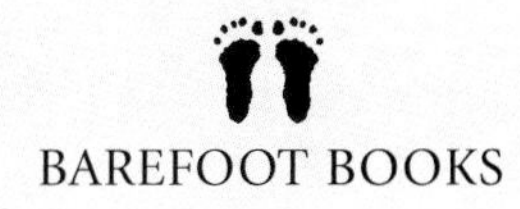

BAREFOOT BOOKS

KATE AND BEN were moving to a new house.

"I hope the garden's got a pond," said Kate, "for being pirates on."

"I hope it's got a cave," said Ben, "for being a caveman in."

When they arrived, they ran out to look. But all the garden had was a crooked old tree.

Ben was cross. "What good's a tree?" he demanded.

"You'll think of something," said Mom.

"But it's just a crooked old tree," argued Kate.

Dad said nothing. He brought out his camera and took a photo of the old, useless tree.

After a few weeks, the tree started to change. It burst into a mass of beautiful, white blossoms.

Every time the spring breezes blew, the tree made snowflakes. Ben became a sled-dog and helped Kate explore the ice, searching for the North Pole.

Dad took a photo.

When the hot days of summer came, Kate and Ben wore their coolest clothes. But the tree grew its thickest, leafiest coat.

Ben was an airman who had crashed his plane in the jungle. Kate was a friendly gorilla who climbed up to rescue him.

Dad took more photos.

When fall came, the tree carried lots of rosy apples.

Kate and Ben were very brave. They had to steal magic apples from the garden of a wicked wizard. The wizard often changed himself into a tiger to scare people away. But Ben and Kate were not afraid at all, and gathered the magic fruit in baskets. Then after lunch, they ate some.

Dad used his camera a lot.

Before long, the tree changed its coat again. Mom said it was borrowing the colors from the sunset.

Whenever the wind blew, the tree dropped bits of sunset all over the garden. Kate and Ben were gold-diggers. They waded out into the dangerous swamps and dug for nuggets of gold. Not even hordes of hungry bears could frighten them away.

Dad took more pictures.

When Hallowe'en came, the tree played tricks on them. It crouched in the wind, pretending to be a witch. Kate and Ben had to trap her inside a ring of their magic apples, to make her spells useless. They were not scared at all.

Dad took a picture to prove it.

One very cold night, Mom said: "Tomorrow we'll have lived here for a whole year. I think we should do something special to celebrate."

"Let's dress up!" said Kate. "I'll be a pirate."

"And I'll be a caveman," said Ben.

In the morning Kate and Ben dressed up. Then they saw that the tree had got dressed up too. It was wearing its loveliest coat ever.

Under the beautiful boughs, the pirate and the caveman pranced happily round and round.

Dad took more photos.

At bedtime, Mom and Dad gave the children a present.

It was a book of photos. It showed all their tree-games: searching for the North Pole, stealing the wizard's apples, digging for gold nuggets, and everything else.

The children were delighted. Then they saw there was a title on the cover. It said, "What Good's a Tree?"

Kate and Ben looked at Mom and Dad.

And everyone laughed.